# STONE ARCH **READERS**

are published by Stone Arch Books
A Capstone Imprint
151 Good Counsel Drive, P.O. Box 669
Mankato, Minnesota 56002
*www.capstonepub.com*

Printed in the United States of America in Melrose Park, Illinois.
092009
005620LKS10

*Library of Congress Cataloging-in-Publication Data*
Crow, Melinda Melton.
Tired trucks / by Melinda Melton Crow ; illustrated by Patrick Girouard.
p. cm. – (Stone Arch readers)
ISBN 978-1-4342-1864-3 (library binding)
ISBN 978-1-4342-2299-2 (pbk.)
[1. Trucks–Fiction.] I. Girouard, Patrick, ill. II. Title.
PZ7.C88536Dr 2010
[E]–dc22
                                    2009034207

Summary: Three truck buddies work hard on the farm.

Art Director: Kay Fraser
Graphic Designer: Hilary Wacholz
Production Specialist: Michelle Biedscheid

Reading Consultants:
Gail Saunders-Smith, Ph.D.
Melinda Melton Crow, M.Ed.
Laurie K. Holland, Media Specialist

## THE MISSING MOUSE

Every time you turn the page,
look for the little mouse.

# TIRED
# TRUCKS

by Melinda Melton Crow

illustrated by Patrick Girouard

STONE ARCH BOOKS
a capstone imprint

This is Green Truck.
This is Yellow Truck.
This is Blue Truck.

The trucks work all day.
They are tired.

The trucks take a nap.
Then they go back to work.

9

"Where is Yellow Truck?"
asks Blue Truck.

Green Truck goes to look for
Yellow Truck.

Blue Truck goes to look for
Yellow Truck, too.

15

Yellow Truck is still sleeping.

"Wake up, Yellow Truck," says
Green Truck.

19

"I am up! I am up!" says
Yellow Truck.

Green Truck goes back to work.

Yellow Truck goes to work, too.

Blue Truck is not there.

Now the trucks have to look
for Blue Truck.

Blue Truck is sleeping.
"We are tired trucks," says
Green Truck.

Follow your favorite TRUCK pals as they learn about the open road.